MURIEL

SAVES STRING

written & illustrated by

DOROTHY WAUGH

jW 357ᴍ

David McKay Company, Inc.   New York, N. Y.

to

DAN

FREDERICK

ESTHER

ALBERT

SIDNEY

CONTENTS

MURIEL
string n. A slender line, thinner than a cord and thicker than a thread.
-Robt's Dict. (top shelf)

MURIEL

SAVES STRING

This is the house where every-thing happened; here and on the farm next door, and in the next town.

This is the house where the Whites live: Mr. White, Mrs. White, Robert, Muriel, and Douglas.

It happened because Muriel always saved string.

When the baker brought the bread to the kitchen door, Muriel saved the string.

When the laundryman brought the laundry and left it on the back porch, Muriel saved the string.

When Muriel's mother came

3

home from shopping and got out of the car in front of the garage door and came in with her arms full of packages, Muriel saved every piece of string—long or short; heavy or light; red or blue or yellow or green or gray or pink or white.

Muriel's big brother Robert said, "What do you save string for? What good is string?"

Muriel's little brother Douglas said, "Saving string is foolish and funny. Nobody but Muriel would ever save string."

But Muriel kept right on saving string. She saved the string from her father's shoe box. She saved the string from her mother's hat box. She saved the string from Robert's chemical set. And when Douglas unwrapped his plastic railroad train Muriel said, "Oh, what a pretty piece of string!" It was purple—her first piece of purple string. She wound it in a little ball and put it in her box of colored string.

Muriel kept her heavy white string in an old writing-paper box. She kept her thinner white string in an old candy box. For her colored string she had a box that soap had come in.

Muriel kept all her string boxes on her own shelf of the bookcase, with her doll Belinda, her sewing basket, and her story books. On the shelf above Muriel's were Robert's chemical set, his stamp album, his baseball, and his hobby books.

On the shelf below Muriel's were Douglas's jumping jack, his toy elephant, his plastic railroad train, and his picture books. Muriel's shelf was the only one where there were boxes labeled STRING.

Whenever Muriel got a new piece of string Robert and Douglas sang, "Muriel sa-aves stri-ing! Muriel sa-aves stri-ing!"

But Muriel paid no attention when they teased her. She wound each piece of string in a neat little bundle and put it away in its proper box: the candy box for thin white string; the writing-paper box for heavy white string; and the box that soap came in for all her colored string.

Every Friday Muriel counted her pieces of string. The Friday when Uncle Rufus came to spend the week end Muriel had 58 pieces of colored string, 72 pieces of heavy white string, and 214 pieces of thinner white string.

TWO ACRES

When Uncle Rufus came to spend the week end, he stopped at Two Acres where the Whites live to say "Hello" to all of them, and then he drove over and left his car in Mr. Briggs's barn next door, because Mr. and Mrs. White and Robert and Muriel and Douglas at their house have only a one-car garage and their own car was in it.

The Whites call their home Two Acres because they built it on two acres they bought from Mr. Briggs. It had been a corner of his farm.

The Whites have an old apple tree in their back yard. It was once part of Mr. Briggs's grandfather's orchard. It is good to climb in. There is a swing hanging from one of the big level limbs. The robin sings in the top branches in the morning—especially in spring when the tree is full of flowers. The brown wren gleans insects from among the buds and twigs. Last summer a pair of bluebirds built their nest in a hole in one old hollow bough. They were as blue as the sky as they flew out of the tree and back.

In front of the Whites' house and in front of Mr. Briggs's house next door there is a long row of maple trees, curving beside the curving road. The robin that built his nest in the maple tree in front of the Whites' front door stole some of Muriel's string last spring right out of her sewing basket when she left in on the front steps. He used the string to help make his nest. Now Muriel always puts her sewing basket away, and she keeps her string in boxes, with the covers on; but in the spring she puts out some of her string for the robins. Uncle Rufus saw some waiting for the robins on the lilac bush by the corner of the house when he came for the week end.

Mr. Briggs on his farm next door lives in a big, old, white house where his father and grandfather and great-grandfather used to live. He thinks the Whites' ranch-type house is funny.

Mr. Briggs has a big red barn. He

has a wagon shed. That is what he calls it because that is what his grandfather called it; but really this is what he has in it now-a-days: a truck; a motor unit

with plough, harrow, and hayrake attachments; his Buick station wagon; and his Ford run-about.

Mr. Briggs has corn-cribs where he keeps the corn he raises until Belle and Brindle, his cows, and Major, his riding horse, eat it up during the winter.

Mr. Briggs has a field for corn, a meadow for hay, a woodlot where he cuts firewood for his fireplaces and lumber to keep his buildings

9

in repair. He has a brook that goes down through the meadow and into the woods.

Mr. Briggs has a large orchard which spreads over the hill. Every fall he picks baskets and baskets and barrels and barrels of apples to send to market.

Mr. Briggs also has a large vegetable garden. Last summer he let Robert and Douglas each have a row of his tomato plants if they would keep them weeded and hoed themselves; and he helped Muriel plant a row of sweet peas in a trench right next to the boys' tomatoes. Only she could cut them; but the bees and humming-birds, and just at dusk sometimes a humming-bird moth, visited them to sip nectar.

When the tomato plants began to grow tall, Mr. Briggs told Robert and Douglas they would need to tie them to strong stakes so they would stand up off the ground where the fruit would be in the sun to grow plump and ripen. For the first time Robert and Douglas needed some string. Muriel said, "I'll lend you some of mine." So Robert and Douglas tied up their tomato plants with some of Muriel's thin white string.

When the sweet pea vines began to grow long, Mr. Briggs cut an armful of brush at the edge of the woods for the vines to climb on. He told Muriel to tie the vines to the brush at first until they began to climb up it by holding on with their curly tendrils. Muriel tied the vines to the brush with some of her thin white string.

Mr. Briggs told Muriel that the more sweet peas she cut the more there would be; so whenever Muriel had time she cut all the sweet peas. She gave her mother some. She gave Mrs. Briggs some. Sometimes she took some to church for the minister to have on the pulpit.

Once when Mr. Briggs was driving into town he told Muriel that if her mother wanted her to go along he would drive around past the county hospital so they could leave some sweet peas there. So Muriel cut all her flowers—five bunches of pink sweet peas; three bunches of white sweet peas; one bunch of red; two bunches of lavender; and three bunches of old-fashioned butterfly sweet peas with pink wings and white breasts. The butterfly sweet peas were her favorites. Mr.Briggs said they used to be his grandmother's favorites, too. Muriel tied all fourteen bunches with her thin white string.

While they drove to the county hospital Mr. Briggs told Muriel that every fall for generations the Briggs men had saved seed of the

butterfly sweet peas; and every spring they had
planted them for their wives. Ever since he could
remember, whenever he went into the kitchen in
July or August, and when he went in now in the
summer from cultivating the corn or making hay,

there on the kitchen window sill above the sink in a
glass bowl almost like a goldfish globe, with the sun
shining through them, were butterfly sweet peas,
and all around them the smell of gingerbread or spice
cake just out of the oven; or New England boiled

dinner, with lots of fresh vegetables; or raspberry jam cooking and bubbling in a big iron kettle on top of the stove.

Mr. Briggs said, the day he and Muriel drove to the county hospital, that the butterfly sweet peas were his favorites, too; and he reached down and drew three out of the bucket and put them in his buttonhole.

Always while Muriel picked her sweet peas Robert and Douglas picked their tomatoes. When only a few tomatoes were ripe, the Whites had them, sliced, for supper. Sometimes they had cottage cheese on the slices. Sometimes they had cole slaw on them. Once for Sunday supper they had Robert's and Douglas's tomatoes stuffed with chicken salad.

When lots of tomatoes were ripe at once, Robert and Muriel and Douglas helped Mrs. White can tomatoes and fix tomato juice for the freezer. The week end Uncle Rufus came Douglas asked if they could have tomato juice the very first thing he came so Uncle Rufus could see how good it was.

So the day Uncle Rufus came and stopped at Two Acres to say "Hello" and then drove over to leave his car in Mr. Briggs's barn, Robert and Muriel drove with him to help him put his car away;

but Douglas stayed and helped his mother get the tomato juice ready for them all to have as soon as Uncle Rufus came back.

Douglas put the glasses on a tray. His mother fixed a pitcher of tomato juice and a plate of cheese crackers. Douglas got out six yellow paper napkins with pictures of animals on them. As soon as Uncle Rufus, Robert, and Muriel came in, Douglas passed the tray—very carefully—even before anyone had time to sit down. Uncle Rufus said the tomato juice was the best he ever tasted.

C H A P T E R

3

UNCLE RUFUS

When Uncle Rufus came for the week end he brought Muriel's mother a box of candy. It was tied with a beautiful piece of . . . *What was it?* Was it string? Was it cord? No! It was ribbon! It was very narrow deep blue ribbon; satin ribbon, as glossy as Uncle Rufus's shiny new blue car which was standing in Mr. Briggs's barn next door.

Muriel asked her mother if she could have the narrow blue ribbon. Her mother said, "Yes." Muriel folded the blue satin ribbon neatly and put it in the soap box with her colored string. Uncle Rufus looked over at the box. In it he saw green string, red string, yellow, brown, gray, blue, orange, pink, and purple string. Robert and Douglas sang, "Muriel sa-aves stri-ing! Muriel sa-aves stri-ing!" They had forgotten that last year they had to borrow some of Muriel's string to tie up their tomato plants.

Uncle Rufus smiled. He looked across the room. "What is that I see over against the wall?" he asked.

Muriel said, "It's my new doll house. Father made it for my birthday. I'll show it to you. This is the living-room. Here is the dining-room and kitchen; they're both one room. Here are the two bedrooms; and the stair hall. I haven't any furniture yet because father is too busy to make furniture."

Uncle Rufus asked, "Can't you make anything for your doll's house yourself?"

Muriel said, "Mother is helping me make curtains for all the windows; white curtains that hang clear to the floor."

Uncle Rufus said, "You could make string rugs. If anyone could find an empty box we could make it into a loom and then you could weave a rug."

Muriel found the empty box her father's new shoes had come in. Uncle Rufus cut the two long sides down a little lower than the ends. He made slits in the ends and stretched thin white string

17

across between them in the slits. "This thin white string is the warp," he explained. "We are going to

weave some colored string in and out in the warp. The colored string will be the woof. The woof and the warp will make the rug because they will hold each other together."

"What colors shall we use?" Muriel asked.

"What do you think will be prettiest?" Uncle Rufus inquired.

"I think pink and gray," Muriel said. So Muriel took all her pink and gray string and a few pieces of white string and wove a pink-and-gray- and-white rug for her doll's house.

They put the rug on the floor of the living-room in the doll's house. "Isn't it pretty?" Muriel asked. "And it's all made entirely of my string."

CAT'S CRADLE

After supper Uncle Rufus said, "Does anyone know how to play cat's cradle?"

Robert said, "No."

Muriel said, "No."

Douglas said, "No."

Uncle Rufus said, "I could teach anyone who had some string."

So Muriel went to the soap box and took out a piece of bright red string and Uncle Rufus taught Muriel how to play cat's cradle.

Robert and Douglas watched. Pretty soon they wanted to play, too.

Muriel said, "I'll lend you some string. Let me see what color I'll let you use."

"Oh," Uncle Rufus said, "it will be better for them to rent the string. If each of them makes a chair for your doll's house, that will pay for using a piece of your string."

So Robert and Douglas got out their knives. They went down cellar and found some empty wooden boxes to use for wood. Then Douglas and Robert spent all evening making two straight chairs for Muriel's doll house.

While the boys made the chairs, Muriel hemmed the curtains for the doll's windows. Uncle Rufus carved a frame for a big overstuffed chair for the doll's living-room. Mrs. White said that some day she would cover it with cotton batting and then with a piece of the gray dotted rayon that was left when she made her best dress.

When Douglas and Robert finished their chairs the children all went to bed. Uncle Rufus promised that he would play cat's cradle with the boys the first thing in the morning, right after they had had breakfast. Muriel said they could use a piece of her green string, but they must have their hands clean, so it wouldn't get soiled.

Douglas asked if they could have tomato juice for breakfast. "Because," he said, "it's from home-grown tomatoes that Robert and I weeded

and picked, so it's especially good."

"Besides," Muriel said, "the tomatoes were tied to the stakes with MY STRING!"

Muriel put the piece of bright red string she and Uncle Rufus had used for playing cat's cradle back in the box the soap had come in. She looked at the narrow glossy blue satin ribbon. "This is the prettiest piece in my whole collection," she remarked, "because it is so blue and so silky." She moved all the pieces of colored string to the edges of the box and put the blue satin ribbon in the middle. "This piece of blue ribbon from the box of candy Uncle Rufus brought to Mother is the queen of my whole string kingdom," she said.

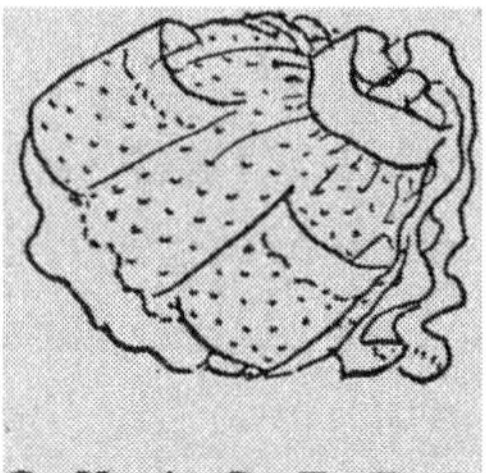

CHAPTER

5

FURNITURE AND FISH-HOOKS

When Mr. White and Uncle Rufus and the children were ready for breakfast on Saturday morning they found Mrs. White in the kitchen getting ready to make cornmeal pancakes. She had on her white apron with yellow dots—the apron Mrs. Briggs had helped Muriel make before Christmas. Muriel had wrapped it in white tissue paper, had tied it with red and green string, and had labeled it with a card she had made herself. The card was shaped like a wreath. In the middle of the wreath Muriel had written "Love to Mother." Then she had put the package on the Christmas tree Mr. Briggs had brought them from his woods. Muriel remembered the Christmas tree now, when she saw her

mother wearing the white apron with the yellow dots.

The apron had two big pockets and a wide bow. "Mother says it's her *best* apron," Muriel remarked.

Uncle Rufus commented, "It's *most* becoming!"

Mr. White said, "*Any* apron has to be pretty when someone so pretty is wearing it."

"Just for that," Mrs. White said, "you two men can each have an extra pancake for breakfast."

For breakfast they had tomato juice, as Douglas had requested. They had homemade maple syrup on their pancakes, and homemade grape jelly from Mr. Briggs's grapes. The children had milk and the grown-ups had coffee.

Right after breakfast Uncle Rufus played cat's cradle with the boys while Muriel helped

her mother do the dishes and make the beds. Then all the children and Uncle Rufus went over to Mr. Briggs's to get the milk and some fresh eggs. They always had Belle's and Brindle's milk and cream, and fresh eggs from Mrs. Briggs's chickens.

It was bright and sunny. Uncle Rufus said, "What a good day to go fishing!"

Robert said, "We haven't any hooks. We can't fish without hooks."

Uncle Rufus said, "We could make hooks out of strong wire."

Douglas said, "We haven't any lines. We can't fish without lines."

Muriel said, "I'll lend you some of my string."

Uncle Rufus said, "It will be better for the boys to rent the string. If they make a table for the doll's house, that will pay for using string for fish lines."

So Robert and Douglas got out their knives. They looked over the wood they had had left after they made the two chairs. Then Douglas and Robert made an oblong table with rounded corners for Muriel's doll's house. It took them all the rest of the morning.

After lunch Mr. White found Uncle Rufus a pair of pliers that had a place on the side for cutting wire. Robert found some strong wire. Then Uncle Rufus and Robert cut and bent four short pieces of wire to make four fish-hooks. Mrs. White gave them a little tin that bouillon cubes had come in to be their box for carrying fish-hooks.

"Now," Uncle Rufus remarked, "we'll have to have some worms for bait."

Robert got the spade and Uncle Rufus and the boys went out to the White's new vegetable garden where they were going to plant lettuce and tomatoes and lima beans as soon as the soil was

dry enough. They dug worms and put them in an empty coffee can. Muriel went down cellar and got four yellow apples to take along when they went fishing in case they got hungry while they were waiting for the fish to bite. She put the apples in a big paper bag.

With the bag of apples, the can of worms, the four fish-hooks in the tin the bouillon

cubes came in, and four pieces of Muriel's string, Uncle Rufus and Douglas and Muriel and Robert started off down the road toward Mr. Briggs's farm next door.

CHAPTER
6

MR. BRIGGS'S BROOK

"Alder wands will be good for fish poles," Uncle Rufus said as he and the children came to the bridge that carried the road over Mr. Briggs's stream.

Uncle Rufus and Robert climbed down the bank. Muriel and Douglas watched from the bridge. Uncle Rufus and Robert cut four straight, strong alder boughs for fish poles.

Then Muriel and her brothers and Uncle Rufus sat on the bridge rail and each fastened a piece of Muriel's string to the end of a pole.

Uncle Rufus said, "We'll keep the hooks in their tin until the last minute, so they won't get hooked into anything."

Muriel asked, "Are we going to fish from the bridge?"

Robert replied, "No. The water is too shallow. Nothing but minnows could swim over all those pebbles in these thin little ripples of water. We have to go where the brook gets narrow and deep."

Uncle Rufus suggested, "I see Mr. Briggs ploughing over in the field where he grew that extra tall corn last year. What if we go over and ask him whether he would mind if we were to fish where the brook runs out of his meadow into his woods."

Muriel said, "That's where we found the yellow violets last spring. Do you remember, Uncle Rufus?"

"Yes," Uncle Rufus said. "I remember."

They went over and waited under the maple trees beside the road and watched Mr. Briggs ploughing toward them on his motor plough, making a straight, even furrow all across the field. He had on his gray work trousers and his brown sweater. The brim of his gray hat was flipped down so it would keep the sun out of his eyes.

When Mr. Briggs came to the end of the furrow next to the road and stopped, ready to

turn the plough around, Uncle Rufus said, "Good morning!"

The children said, "Hi!"

Mr. Briggs said, "Fine spring day."

Uncle Rufus said, "Your soil looks pretty mellow there. Just about dried out enough, after the late snow, for the plough, isn't it?"

"Just about right," Mr. Briggs said.

Uncle Rufus asked, "Would you have any objections if we four went fishing in your brook down near where it runs out of the meadow into the woods?"

"No, I'd have no objections," Mr. Briggs answered. "It's only those city folks that tramp on the fields and break branches and leave litter around that I object to."

"We'll be careful," Douglas said.

So they climbed over the fence, scrambled down the bank, and set off to fish in Mr. Briggs's brook.

WATERFALLS

AND POOLS

Uncle Rufus and the children walked along the bank of the stream at the edge of the meadow, heading toward the woods.

A yellow warbler, like a little fleck of bright joy, flitted along ahead of them, singing and singing. He darted from a clump of pussy-willow to a leaning crab-apple tree; he glided from the crab-apple tree to a tall dry last year's weed; he winged buoyantly in a wide high curve from the tall brown weed to another fringe of pussy-willows farther along the brook—always keeping teasingly ahead. Then he soared lightly into the air and over their heads and back in a moment to where they and he had started from together.

33

Uncle Rufus and Muriel and her brothers went on along the brook. They saw fresh mint leaves springing at the very margin of the water. They saw a small turtle sunning himself on a wet log at the brink of the stream. They came to the place where the younger trees were pushing out ahead of the older trees at the edge of the woods.

There they could see the rill that was coming down through the woodland to join the brook that was curving from the sunlit meadow into the shade of the thicket.

"Now," Robert said, "the brook is wide enough and deep enough for trout."

They went on into the edge of the woodland. They passed seven little waterfalls where the water fell tumbling, singing over the stones. Then they came to a chain of quiet pools where witch-hazel branches hung out over the water. "Here is a good place to fish," Uncle Rufus said.

Muriel and Douglas sat on a big stone. Robert leaned against a tall tulip tree. Uncle Rufus tossed his yellow sweater onto the ground and stood where the bank jutted out between two shadowy pools. Last year's grass hung over the margin of the water, making secret shelters where fish could hide.

They all tied their hooks to their lines. They all threaded worms on their hooks. They

all lowered their hooks quietly into the water.

They waited—not even whispering; trying to be quieter and more patient than the fish.

After a while Muriel whispered excitedly, "Oh, I think I have a bite!"

She pulled up her line. "Oh!" she said sadly. What she had caught was only a leaf that had been floating down the stream under water! She let her hook drop into the pool again.

U. S. 941510   *35*

After a while Douglas said, "I'm going to cast." He flipped his line out of the water with a jerk of his pole. The hook flew up in the air and caught in the dogwood branches above his head.

Robert said, "There's no use to cast with that stiff rod and that heavy hook, and just string!"

Uncle Rufus added, "Casting is for a delicate, flexible rod and a strong, slender line, and trout flies." He untangled Douglas's line from the branches.

Douglas dropped his hook and worm back into the pool. They all waited and waited.

Suddenly Robert gave a quick upward twitch to his pole. Then everyone could see that something was tugging at his line. With one strong flip Robert landed a small flopping trout on the bank beside the stream. They all stood and admired it.

They fished a while longer. Then they ate their apples. A phoebe called and called and darted out above the water to catch insects. Finally Uncle Rufus looked at his watch and said, "We'd better go."

When he went to pick up his

yellow sweater he saw it move. Something small was jumping under it. "I believe I've caught a frog," he said.

"Are we going to keep it?" asked Douglas.

"Some people eat frogs' legs," Uncle Rufus said.

"Oh, let it go," Muriel cried.

So Uncle Rufus lifted his sweater and a slim green frog leaped into the pool with a splash and was gone. They watched the circles he left

rippling across the surface of the water. The circles grew wider and wider till they ruffled the whole pool and disappeared at the rocking water's edge. When the pool was quiet and dark again, and all the shimmering silver ripples were gone, Unce Rufus and Robert and Muriel and Douglas picked up their poles and lines, and the coffee can (and dumped the rest of the worms out into the water) and put their hooks back into the tin their mother gave them for fishhooks. They tore up the paper bag and soaked the pieces in the water so they wouldn't blow around on Mr. Briggs's land. They weighted them under a stone in the water's edge. Then they started home.

C H A P T E R
8

GRAY CAR

As Robert, Douglas, Muriel, and Uncle Rufus followed beside the brook back toward the road they saw a gray car coming around the hill.

They were just scrambling up the bank to the bridge when the car came along beside them and stopped. A thin man with red hair asked, "What have you got there?" He was looking at Robert's little fish.

Robert replied, "A trout. I'm the only one that caught one." He held it up proudly.

"Have you got a fishing license?" the man asked.

The children looked surprised and turned to Uncle Rufus.

Uncle Rufus said to the man with red hair, "Are you a game warden?"

"Yes," the man answered, turning back his plaid lumber jacket to show his official badge.

Uncle Rufus asked, "Do children have to have licenses? Are licenses required for fishing on a next-door neighbor's land when he has given permission?"

Mr. Briggs, who had finished ploughing and was walking back from the tool shed, came over to the roadside fence and stood with his foot on a rail. He kept his mouth very straight.

The warden looked at Mr. Briggs. Then he looked at Uncle Rufus. He said, "Better inform yourself on those matters *before* fishing, not after." He stepped on the gas and drove off down the road and out of sight around the curve.

Mr. Briggs and Uncle Rufus smiled. Douglas asked, "Why did the game warden stop us when he didn't do anything to us?"

Mr. Briggs replied, "I think he wanted to be sure that you would remember that there are laws and that everyone is required to know them. As a matter of fact, it's against the law in this state for anyone but the owner or his immediate family to fish on his land without a license, permission or no permission."

Uncle Rufus commented, "Then I guess I was the only one who was breaking the law.

I'm pretty sure that children under fourteen don't have to have licenses."

Douglas asked, "What if the warden had arrested you, Uncle Rufus?"

"I would have had to pay a fine," Uncle Rufus answered.

Robert asked, "Isn't it his duty to arrest you?"

"His major duty," Uncle Rufus replied, "is to keep the law from being broken. If he thinks that a warning is going to do that as well as an arrest, then he just gives a warning."

Robert held up his trout for Mr. Briggs to see.

Mr. Briggs said, "Almost half a mouthful apiece you've got there."

"Anyway," Muriel said, "we had fun."

They went home and told their mother, "Muriel caught a leaf. Douglas caught a branch. Uncle Rufus almost caught a green frog. Robert caught a trout. Here it is for dinner."

Muriel said, "Now give me back my string, because it was only rented."

STRING AND
MORE STRING

The week end when Uncle Rufus and Robert, Muriel, and Douglas played cat's cradle and went fishing in Mr. Briggs's stream, came to an end; but Uncle Rufus promised that he would come again in June.

"Make it that special week end we talked about," Muriel urged, "because that is when Luke's Boys' Club has its Boys' Fair. You said you'd go with us, you know."

"I won't forget," Uncle Rufus promised. "I'll make it that special week end."

Luke was Muriel's cousin who lived in the next town.

Sure enough, when June and the

week end for the Boys' Fair came, on Saturday morning a blue roadster drove up and stopped in front of Two Acres. Uncle Rufus got out and said "Hello" to all the Whites. Then the children drove over with him to leave his car in Mr. Briggs's barn.

As they were walking back Uncle Rufus said, "What a wonderful windy day! What grand weather this would be for flying a kite."

"Uncle Rufus," Douglas asked, "do you know how to make a kite?"

"Yes," Uncle Rufus said.

Robert asked, "Muriel, if Douglas and I make a stove and a bookcase for your doll's house, will you let us use some of your string for a kite?"

"Yes," Muriel said.

So Douglas and Robert got out their knives and the wood that was left after they made the two chairs, the table, and also two beds and a bureau that they had made since (because they wanted some string—to keep—to tie up their this year's tomato plants).

They made a stove and a bookcase for the doll's house. They painted the stove white with some paint their father had had left after he finished making the doll's house and painting it.

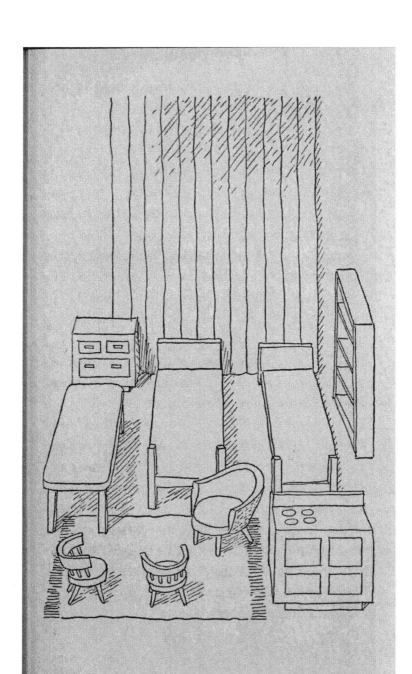

Then after lunch Uncle Rufus helped them make a kite.

They took some slender strips of wood and notched them and bound them together with some of Muriel's light-weight white string to make a kite frame. Then they looped a piece of Muriel's string around the outside of the frame. They covered the frame with newspaper.

For the leader that they were going to hold the kite by when it flew off up to the sky they used all of Muriel's heavy white string. They found a strong stick for a reel and wound the leader on the reel.

They used a piece of Muriel's green string for the kite-tail. They tied small oblongs of newspaper into the green string for the tail.

When the kite was finished they all went out on the hillside toward Mr. Briggs's barn. The wind was strong. The clouds were rolling and white. Douglas and Muriel and Robert and Uncle Rufus stood near the end of the barn. They could hear Mr. Briggs's cows, Brindle and Belle, mooing from their stanchions. They could hear Mr. Briggs's riding horse, Major, stamping his hoof in his stall. Swallows were skimming in and out of the big barn door and off over the meadow.

46

Uncle Rufus held the kite as high in the air as he could reach, with the wind blowing against it. Robert took the reel and ran into the wind as hard as he could run, unwinding the leader as he ran.

The kite rose a little way. Then it dipped crazily and dived to the ground. Uncle Rufus said, "It needs a longer tail to steady it."

Robert said, "I guess we have to go back for more string."

Muriel felt in her sweater pocket. Her only piece of purple string was there. She had taken it out of the soap box before they made the kite-tail because she didn't want them to take her only purple piece. But now she said, "You can use this piece." She gave Uncle Rufus the purple string.

"But we have to have paper to tie into it," Uncle Rufus reminded them.

"Oh," Douglas said. "Mr. Briggs has a pile of old newspapers in his tool shed. He uses them to clean the earth from the ploughshare and from the blade of his shovel or his spade or his hoe or the teeth of his rake when he comes in from work. He won't mind if I take a piece or two. I'll get us some from there."

Douglas got some newspaper from

47

Mr. Briggs's tool shed. Robert tied a purple tail to the green tail of the kite. Then Uncle Rufus held the

kite as high as he could reach, facing the wind. Robert ran into the wind, unwinding the leader from the reel as he ran. The kite rose and rose, hardly diving at all. It rode, strong and steady, high on the wind.

When the sun caught it, it was as white as the billowy clouds. When it turned so its shadow face looked down at them, it shimmered with lavender against the blue sky. Douglas said, "I want to fly it."

Robert replied, "The wind is too strong. You couldn't hold it."

"Yes, I could," Douglas said.

Uncle Rufus said, "Perhaps Douglas and Muriel together could hold it."

They tried.

The wind blew boisterously.

The kite tugged, hard, high above the barn.

Douglas and Muriel held on very tight and leaned back because the kite was jerking to get away.

Suddenly Douglas tripped over a hummock in the grass. Muriel tried to catch him. They both fell. They lost hold of the reel. When they got up they saw the kite flying wild, the leader dragging, the reel hitting the roof of the barn and bouncing off as the kite flew far and far away. Robert and

Uncle Rufus were running across the hill. But the kite was gone.

They all stood and watched.

Finally the kite shivered, dived, and then came fluttering down toward the fields. As it fell, the dragging leader was caught in the top of an elm tree. There the kite dangled above the ground.

Robert went running along the edges of the fields, climbing the fences, rushing toward the elm tree where the kite was caught.

Uncle Rufus and Douglas and Muriel saw Robert shinny up the trunk of the elm. They saw him pull in the kite and untangle the leader from the branches. They saw him drop down from the tree with the kite.

When he came back he showed them that the reel and the end of the leader were gone; and the purple end of the tail was missing. "My favorite piece of string," Muriel said.

They went home with the kite and part of Muriel's string. At supper, after they had all bowed their heads and said the blessing aloud together—*Bless the Lord, O my soul, and forget not all His benefits*—while Mr. White was carving the meat loaf and Mrs. White was serving the creamed potatoes, the children told their parents all about

how Robert flew the kite so high on the wind that it looked like a mere speck; how Douglas and Muriel tried to fly it; how Douglas tripped and he and Muriel both tumbled down; how the kite flew off by itself and the leader dragged the reel over the roof of the barn; how the reel and part of the leader and part of the kite-tail got lost.

Douglas told his father, "We lost Muriel's favorite piece of purple string."

"Maybe," Mr. White said, "you'd better make her a piano for her doll's house in payment."

"That's too hard," Douglas said, ". . . unless someday you'll help us."

CHAPTER
10

OFF TO THE FAIR

Muriel and her mother were just bringing in the applesauce and cookies for dessert when the telephone rang. Someone wanted to speak to Robert. It was Luke.

"Robert," Luke said, "remember I told you I'm showing my model airplanes at the Fair this evening. I just called the manager of the Fair and asked if my cousins from out of town could show theirs. He said that any boy can show anything he made himself. So bring yours, too. Be sure to be here by seven-thirty because we have to fill out entry blanks and put our planes in place and the judges are going to judge at eight o'clock. There are going to be lots of entries because everyone has found out there's no rule against out-of-town boys exhibiting."

Robert, Muriel, and Douglas all helped wash the supper dishes and put them away. Then they and their father and mother and Uncle Rufus got ready to drive over to their cousin Luke's house to go to the Boys' Fair with him.

When they had put Robert's and Douglas's airplanes in the car Muriel said, "Can't we take my doll's house, too, so we can show the furniture Robert and Douglas made?"

"Why, what a good idea!" Mr. White said.

So they put the doll's house in the trunk in the back of the car and they all drove to Luke's house. Then they went on with Luke and his father and mother to the Boys' Fair.

When they got to the Town Hall there were boys everywhere. Streams of people were going up the steps and into the big front door. A sign said BOYS FAIR. . . ALL WELCOME.

They went in.

Just inside the door sat two women at a table. "Fill out your entry blanks here," they said.

Luke and Robert and Douglas all filled out entry cards for model airplanes. Then

Robert and Douglas filled out a card for doll's furniture. They had to put down their names and ages,

and a line saying what they were exhibiting.

When their entry cards were ready the women said, "Take your exhibits into the big hall on the left. Model airplanes have to hang from the wires down the two sides of the hall. Other entries are to be arranged on the tables in the middle."

Douglas said to Robert, "How can we hang our planes? We haven't any string."

One of the women said, "I'm sorry we can't help you. We thought we had plenty of string; but there have been so many more planes entered than we expected, it is all used up already."

Muriel looked at Uncle Rufus. They both smiled. Muriel said, "You can use my string. I brought it with me, just in case. Uncle Rufus told me to."

"Whew!" Douglas said. "What luck!"

BEFORE

EIGHT O'CLOCK

In the exhibit hall dozens of boys were arranging scores of exhibits. Most of the exhibits were model planes, but in the middle of the room where Uncle Rufus and Mr. White were helping Muriel set up her doll's house there were tool chests, traps, stools, book-ends; wooden birds painted in the colors of familiar native birds the children knew; there were shoe-shine kits, cookie cutters, building blocks, bird houses, a game board, a stepladder, and a clothes drier; there were toy boats, and trucks, and derricks; and two toy automobiles big enough for a five-year-old to ride in.

"Don't take time to look at things now," Robert said, "or we won't have our exhibits

in place before the judges come."

When he and Luke and Douglas had their planes all hung from the wires with Muriel's string and everyone had looked at them and admired them, Muriel said, "Now come and look at my doll's house."

There on the doll's living-room floor was the pink-and-gray-and-white rug. There were the two chairs and the oblong table; the two beds and the bureau; the white stove and the bookcase. In all the windows fresh new white curtains were hanging. In the overstuffed chair sat Belinda in her best green-and-brown checked dress, looking at the ceiling. Beside the overstuffed chair was a card. It was one of Mr. White's business cards that he had happened to have in his pocket; but only the back of it showed, where Mr. White had lettered with his fountain pen in very little letters, "This chair is the only piece of furniture not made by the exhibitors."

While they were saying how fine Muriel's doll house looked, a loud bell clanged. They all turned around. At the end of the room stood a big man in a very black suit and a very white shirt. He had a pearl-gray tie. He was very tall and very wide and through the middle he was very thick.

His hair was extra black. His

glasses were extra shiny. His ears were small. His nose was large. Luke whispered, "He's the mayor. His name is Mayor Carlton. The postman's son told my friend Reuben's brother that Mayor Carlton eats nothing but snails; but I don't believe it; do you?"

Everybody stopped talking. The room grew very quiet. Mayor Carlton's voice was as deep as a bass drum. He said:

"Ladies and gentlemen! I am delighted to see so many happy faces here before me

this evening. It is a great event for our town to have the Boys' Fair here in our own Town Hall. I, personally, feel it a very hopeful sign that the young men, if I may call them that, of our coming generation, are so ingenious with their hands and minds as these exhibits we have before us prove them to be."

Mayor Carlton took a long breath and looked all around. Then he continued:

"I want now to ask you all to withdraw to the adjoining hall and to be seated there so the judges may be undisturbed as they weigh the relative merits of the exhibits which have been arranged for their attention. As soon as the judges have

determined which entries are to be singled out for award they will place a yellow ribbon rosette on the third prize entry, and a red ribbon rosette on the second entry; but the blue ribbon rosette which I am holding here—" he held it up for everyone to see—"will be presented in person to the winner of first place."

Mayor Carlton cleared his throat loudly, as if it were growing rough. His glasses gleamed. He went on:

"The judges, after the decisions have been reached, will follow us to the adjoining hall. There we will call the winner of first place to the platform to receive the blue ribbon in person. The photographer from our local *Morning Eagle* will photograph the presentation."

When Mayor Carlton had finished speaking everyone hurried to find seats in the adjoining hall—everyone except Mayor Carlton and the three judges. Mayor Carlton walked slowly and sedately. He didn't hurry at all, because there was a seat saved for him on the platform. The three judges stayed behind to judge.

Luke and Robert and Muriel and Douglas looked at the three judges.

One was a very short, fat man in a gray-green suit with a pink tie. He was nearly bald. Luke said, "He's an insurance agent. He is very good-natured. I hope he'll like my planes."

One was a gaunt man with sparkling black eyes and rumpled hair. His face was as brown and wrinkled as his suit. Robert said, "I think

he knows mechanical details. I hope he'll like my biggest bomber with the pliofilm turret."

The third judge was an elderly man with white hair and a trim, small, white mustache. His gray suit was sharply pressed. A fresh, clean white handkerchief with its four corners arranged to show their points, was peeking above the edge of his breast pocket. His tie was soft, silky brown with a small pattern in silvery gray. His eyes were gray, pleasant, and keen. When the Mayor spoke to him he smiled. Douglas said, "He's going to like my smallest plane best, because it's the neatest. I hope he votes for me to get the first prize."

In the adjoining hall Mayor Carlton climbed the three steps to the platform and sat down in the high-backed chair. Beside him was a stand with a pitcher of water and a glass. Mayor Carlton poured himself a glass of water and sat with his hands folded across his stomach. His glasses were shining. His little ears were pink. His large nose cast a long shadow down over his chin.

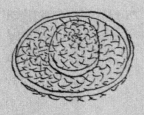

STRAWS AND SONGS

The cousins and their parents and Uncle Rufus took up almost a whole row of seats in the adjoining hall. Nearby they saw Mr. and Mrs. Briggs, who had driven over to see everything at the Boys' Fair.

While the audience waited, a boys' quartet sang. They were all dressed like farmers. They didn't wear the kind of clothes Mr. Briggs wears, but the kind of clothes farmers in cartoons wear. They had big straw hats and plaid shirts and blue overalls. On their feet they wore high boots. When they came out on the platform they all had long pieces of straw in their mouths. They took the straws out when they sang and put them back when they finished, while everybody clapped. They called themselves The Four Farmers Quartet.

Luke said that two of the boys were brothers. Their grandfather had taught them

some old, old songs he used to sing when he was in college. Those were the songs they sang.

They sang about Uncle Josh. *"When the corn is ripe and ready for to husk, Way down on the farm . . ."*

The two tallest boys were standing in the middle. The boy on the left end, who had yellow curly hair, kept acting gay and funny. He beat time with his foot, and sometimes with his head. He gestured with his hands and overworked his face and swayed to the music. He made everybody feel gay.

One of the tall boys in the middle was thin and dark and solemn. He stood as stiff as a stick and never moved a muscle of his face except barely to make the words. He kept his shoulders square and level, and he kept his head as stiff as a frozen icicle. He looked very solemn; but when they sang, *"Lots of fun for you and me, Way down on the farm. . . ."* he winked at Muriel.

Everybody laughed.

Luke whispered, "Ah-Ha!"

Muriel said, "It's just because I happen to be near the front."

Luke said, "Oh, no! It's because you're so charming."

Uncle Rufus smiled.

Muriel blushed. "Luke loves to tease," she said.

When the Four Farmers Quartet finished singing about Uncle Josh everyone clapped and clapped. Then the boys sang, *"Put on your old gray bonnet . . . And I'll hitch Old Dobbin to the*

67

shay." After that they sang *"Sweet Adeline, say you'll be mine . . . Way down yonder in the old cornfield For you I pine. . . ."*

The audience clapped so much after *Sweet Adeline* that the tall, solemn boy stepped forward and held one finger straight up. When the people were all quiet he said, "Everyone knows the words to *Sweet Adeline*. Let's try that again, all together."

Then he stepped back into his place in the row; but he still held up one finger and led the music with it.

Everybody sang. Luke kept putting in words of his own:

Way down yonder in the Briggs cornfield
For you I pine.
Sweeter than a puppy to a jumping flea.
I love you; say you love me.
Meet me in the shade of your old apple
*   tree-ee-ee;*
Or out beside your old tomato vi-ine!

Just as they finished singing, while all the people in the audience were settling back in their chairs, the photographer from the *Morning Eagle* came striding up the aisle. He had a camera and flashlights. He crouched down and focused the

camera on the mayor. Then he stood up and waited.

Finally the judges came in. The short one in the gray-green suit with the pink tie and a black-and-gray-and-white plaid vest, who had only one button on his coat and kept twirling it between his thumb and finger, went up and passed Mayor Carlton a slip of yellow paper.

YELLOW,

RED, AND BLUE

Mayor Carlton looked at the paper the judge had passed to him. He walked to the edge of the platform. To himself he read the paper again. Then he said:

"Ladies and gentlemen! I now have the pleasure to make known the decisions of the judges as to the winners in this year's Boys' Fair. But first let me thank the three men who have so kindly served as our judges this evening; and let me thank the many others who have given of their time and talents to make this affair such a happy success, not forgetting those who worked on the plans; who served on committees; who registered our entrants tonight at the door; nor the Four Farmers Quartet which has added so much to our evening's enjoyment."

The Mayor picked up the glass of water and took a short drink. Then he went on, the

yellow paper still waiting forgotten in his hand:

"Let me remark, too, that I consider this occasion a bright spot in the year here in our town. I am convinced that this annual Boys' Fair is one of the great and significant events in our community life. What our boys learn today our men will know tomorrow."

The Mayor beamed a moment at the audience. Then he looked down at the paper. He said:

"I have the honor to announce that the yellow ribbon rosette, for third place in this year's exhibit, has been awarded for a fine display of model planes, predominantly jets. These were entered in competition by . . ." The Mayor looked at the paper once more. "Luke Meadows," he said.

Luke gasped.

Everybody clapped.

"Whew!" Douglas exclaimed. Robert leaned over and shook Luke's hand. All the people sitting nearby whispered congratulations. Muriel confided happily, "Luke, I always knew you were a winner!" Uncle Rufus's face broke into a wide grin.

After a moment the Mayor continued:

"The red ribbon rosette, for second award, has been placed by the judges on a miniature automobile built and entered by . . ." He glanced at his memorandum. "By Gerald Green."

Luke exclaimed, "Ha! Gerald Green is Reuben's brother. You know, the one that told us about the snails."

The clapping was loud. Everyone was smiling. Muriel saw Mr. Briggs lean forward and congratulate a man sitting in front of him. "That," Luke whispered, "is Reuben's and Gerald's father. He sold Mr. Briggs the farm truck he hauls apples to market in."

The Mayor waited patiently for the audience to quiet down. He stood with both hands folded over the yellow paper. When all was hushed he took a deep breath.

"And now," he said, "to crown our highly successful evening it is my real pleasure and great privilege to name the winner of first place and to present to him in person our highest honor, the blue ribbon rosette."

He consulted the judges' notes. "The winner . . ." he began, and stopped. He took off his glasses, wiped them, put them on again, and referred to the memorandum once more. "No," he said, "not the winner, but the *winners* of first place are two brothers. They have been singled out for this paramount recognition for doll's furniture—which I hope you will all take time to examine. First place goes to Robert and Douglas White. Will they please step up to the platform?"

There was a storm of applause. Robert and Douglas were very excited. Luke was pumping their hands up and down. "You lucky stiffs!" he said. Muriel and Uncle Rufus and all the rest in their row were overwhelmed with surprise and delight that one family should have *two* awards.

The Mayor peered over his glasses into the audience. "Will Robert and Douglas White please come forward?" he repeated.

Robert and Douglas stumbled up the aisle to the platform. They stood self-consciously beside the Mayor. The photographer from the *Morning Eagle* took his camera from under his arm.

Mayor Carlton boomed out, to be heard above the roar of the audience, "I want to say once more what pleasure it affords me to award this ... this ... this ...."

Mayor Carlton was looking for the blue ribbon rosette. He couldn't find it. He felt in all his pockets. He peered all around. He hunted everywhere. Robert looked uneasy. Douglas was worried. Mayor Carlton felt in his inside and his outside pockets again. He looked down at the floor. He looked under the chair where he had been sitting and under

the table where the pitcher of ice water stood.

"But I had it just a moment ago," he said in a loud, worried whisper. He went through his pockets for the third time. Then he said to the photographer, "Can't we dispense with the ribbon?"

The photographer was shocked. "Blue ribbon winners and no blue ribbon!" he exclaimed. "Who ever heard of such a thing? The ribbon's important to the picture. Without it we just have a couple of boys—any boys; anywhere. It's the ribbon that marks them as winners."

The Mayor sighed a deep sigh from the very bottom of his shining black boots. "But the ribbon has vanished," he moaned; "has completely disappeared. I can't make a blue ribbon out of thin air."

The photographer shrugged his shoulders. "Sorry!" he murmured apologetically. He put his camera back under his arm.

Douglas and Robert were most embarrassed. Mayor Carlton clenched his fingers tightly and unclenched them again. He opened his mouth and then closed it. He ran his hands hopelessly through his hair.

Suddenly Mrs. White leaned over and whispered to Uncle Rufus. Quickly he passed her his knife. Urgently she whispered to Muriel. Muriel whisked her narrow blue satin ribbon out of the soap box. With a sharp stroke Mrs. White cut the

ribbon in two. She hurriedly tied two pretty rosettes. "Take these up to Mayor Carlton," she said to Muriel.

Muriel hurried to the platform and reached up with the two rosettes.

Mayor Carlton was mopping his brow and his neck with his rumpled handkerchief. When he saw what Muriel was holding up he looked most astonished. He could see that what she was offering him was not the one rosette he had lost, but two beautiful twin rosettes made of narrow, shiny,

blue satin ribbon. A broad smile spread over his face.

"How ever did you happen to have this ribbon with you?" Mayor Carlton questioned Muriel.

"I saved it with my string," Muriel answered.

"Do you save string?" inquired Mayor Carlton.

Douglas and Robert replied, "Muriel *always* saves string!"

Mayor Carlton exclaimed, "And what a lucky thing for us!" He looked at the gleaming rosettes in his hands. Then he looked at Muriel. "My dear young lady," he said, "may I ask your name?"

"Muriel White," Muriel said.

"Well!" the photographer from the *Morning Eagle* broke in. "If my guess is right, you must be sister to these blue ribbon winners!"

"Yes," Muriel smiled. "It's my doll's house they made the furniture for."

"In that case," the photographer observed, "I'd like to have you in the picture, too."

"A most excellent idea," agreed the Mayor.

"Can I be holding Belinda?" Muriel asked.

"Is Belinda your doll?"

"Yes. She's sitting in the exhibition hall in my doll house in the overstuffed chair and she has on her very best dress."

"All right," the photographer said. "Run and get her."

Muriel ran and got Belinda.

Mayor Carlton pinned the lustrous blue ribbon rosettes on Robert and Douglas. "We look like knights after a king has decorated them," Robert said when he saw how gorgeous the rosettes looked.

Muriel proudly stepped between her brothers, holding Belinda. Mayor Carlton stood behind her, the light shining on his glasses and his large nose casting a wide shadow on his chin. The photographer from the *Morning Eagle* squatted down, squinted through the finder on his camera, twisted this way and that, and took their picture. It

was because Luke was making a funny face at them that they were all grinning in the picture.

The photographer closed his camera and marched away, down the aisle and out the big door. The Mayor held up his hand for attention.

"Before our evening draws to a close," he suggested, "I feel everyone here would like a special opportunity. I want to ask if all those who wish to express appreciation to Miss Muriel White, this lovely young lady who saves string, who has saved the day for us here with her blue ribbon rosettes . . . Will everyone who cares to express appreciation to this charming young lady rise for a moment in her honor?"

There was a deafening roar of applause. Everyone stood up, clapping and calling. Mr. and Mrs. Briggs waved. Luke whistled. The audience

clapped and clapped, Uncle Rufus loudest of all. The tall boy from the Farmers' Quartette who had winked at Muriel during the singing shouted, "Yippee!"

Muriel stood between her brothers, smiling and blushing. Belinda looked proudly up into her face.

Ever since the second week end when Uncle Rufus visited at Two Acres—not the week end when they learned to play cat's cradle and went fishing in Mr. Briggs's brook, but the one when they flew the kite on the hill beside the red barn, and went to the Boys' Fair— every time the baker brings the bread Robert and Douglas and Muriel *all* race to get the string. Whenever the laundryman brings the laundry, they all rush to see which can get the string. And whenever Mrs. White comes home from shopping with her arms full of packages, before she even gets her hat off Robert and Muriel and Douglas have agreed among themselves which of them will have *this* piece of string, and which will have *that* piece of string. They *all* have boxes marked STRING on their shelves on the bookcase, and now-a-days Robert and Douglas, as you can very well believe, never—no never—sing:

"Muriel sa-ves stri-ing!"
"Muriel sa-ves stri-ing!"

1822

CPSIA information can be obtained
at www.ICGtesting.com
Printed in the USA
BVHW080011141221
623924BV00007B/562